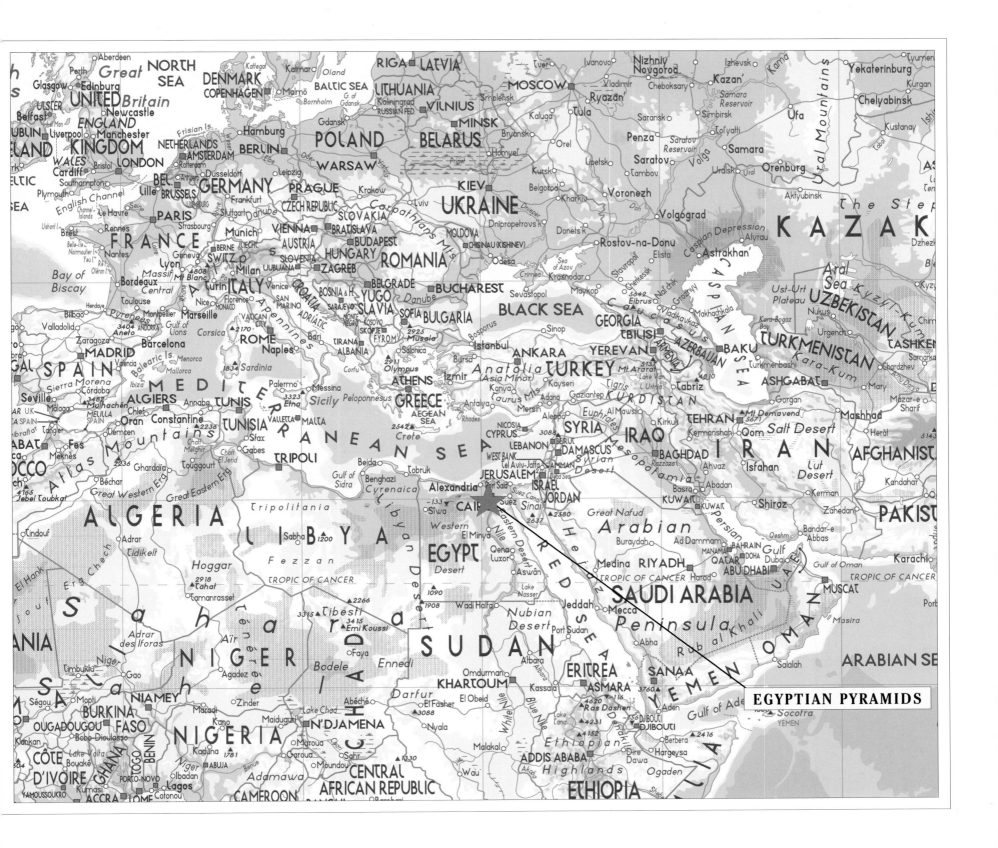

EGYPTIAN PYRAMIDS

Published by Creative Education
123 South Broad Street
Mankato, Minnesota 56001

Creative Education is an imprint of The Creative Company.

Designed by Stephanie Blumenthal
Production design by The Design Lab
Art direction by Rita Marshall

Photographs by Corbis (Bruce Adams; Eye Ubiquitous, Paul Almasy, Archivo Iconografico,
S.A., Bettmann, Tibor Bognár, Christie's Images, Hugh Clark; Frank Lane Picture Agency,
Mark Cooper, Abbie Enock; Travel Ink, Paul Hardy, Larry Lee Photography, Jean-Pierre Lescourret,
Ludovic Maisant, Aladin Abdel Naby/Reuters, David A. Northcott, Premium Stock, Jose Fuste Raga,
Carmen Redondo, Roger Ressmeyer, Reuters, Rykoff Collection, Paul Schermeister, Leonard de Selva,
Craig Tuttle, Underwood & Underwood, Sandro Vannini, Ron Watts, Roger Wood),
Getty Images (Doug Armand, Jochem D Wijnands)

Printed in the United States of America

Library of Congress Cataloging-in-Publication Data

Peterson, Sheryl.
Egyptian pyramids / by Sheryl Peterson.
p. cm. — (Ancient wonders of the world)
Includes index.
ISBN 1-58341-359-6
1. Pyramids—Egypt—Juvenile literature. I. Title. II. Series.

DT63.P48 2005   932—dc22   2004055266

First edition

2 4 6 8 9 7 5 3 1

ANCIENT WONDERS OF THE WORLD

Egyptian Pyramids

SHERYL PETERSON

CREATIVE EDUCATION

Whether seen in their entirety or block-by-block, the pyramids of Egypt are awe-inspiring. Built by hand more than four millenia ago, the pyramids stand today as relics of a powerful ancient society.

Up from the shimmering heat of the desert sands they soar, their majestic peaks pointed toward the heavens. For thousands of years, the Egyptian pyramids have beckoned travelers to marvel at the age of the pharaohs. These magnificent tombs, where stone meets sky, took years to build and were filled with treasures to assist the kings in their journey through the **afterlife**. Scientists, architects, and scholars continue to wonder how ancient builders acquired the extraordinary knowledge and materials needed to build these gigantic, mysterious structures that seem to defy the effects of time.

An old Arab saying states: "Man fears time—time fears the pyramids." It suggests that people are afraid of time because it brings old age and eventually death, but that time does not seem to affect the pyramids. They stand today as they have for more than 4,500 years.

AGE OF THE PHARAOHS

Five thousand years ago, one of the greatest civilizations of the ancient world was born in Egypt along the banks of the Nile River. Egypt has been called the "Gift of the Nile," for the waters of this long, snaking river allowed the otherwise dry land to become a cradle of prosperity. From the beginning of the Old Kingdom (the rule of royal families from 2575 to 2130 B.C.), the power of Egypt expanded. Government became more centralized and spurred an era of unbroken rule by all-powerful pharaohs, or kings.

Daily life in ancient Egypt revolved around the Nile and the fertile soil along its banks. The yearly flooding of the river enriched the soil and brought good harvests and wealth to the land. People grew most of their own food, including barley, wheat, grapes, and pomegranates. Another crop, flax, was grown to produce linen for lightweight clothing that kept people cool. In Egypt's hot, desert climate, all homes, even the pharaohs' palaces, were made of mud brick, a natural form of air-conditioning.

As the Old Kingdom grew in power, so did the pharaohs. The kings were considered to be gods descended from the sun god, Ra, and lived in palaces and temples built to worship them. When a pharaoh took the

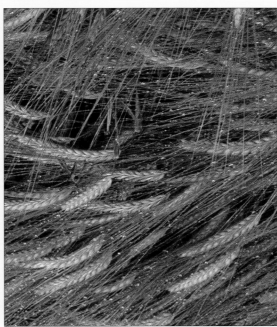

Ancient Egyptians called the fertile banks of the Nile River the "black land" because of the dark soil brought by the river's annual flooding. The Nile River valley was the only area of the country where crops such as grapes (top), flax (bottom left), and barley (bottom right) could be grown.

Egyptians were experts at preserving the dead as mummies. In the 1990s, many mummies were unwrapped for scientific study. Today, special scanners are used to see inside mummies without causing damage.

The god Anubis (right), who took the form of a jackal, was believed to guide the dead through the underworld.

throne, he would begin immediately to plan his place for eternity.

Egyptians believed that it was important to be buried properly, which would allow them to live again in the afterlife. Most people were probably buried in the desert, wrapped in simple cloth. Kings and very wealthy people were often wrapped as **mummies** and buried in tombs called *mastabas*. This early type of tomb had an underground burial chamber and an offering chapel above ground.

With the development of stone architecture around 2780 B.C., the first pyramid built as a tomb was constructed by King Djoser at Saqqara, near the city of Memphis. It still stands today and is known as a step pyramid, since it consists of six *mastabas* piled on top of each other like steps. Inside is a honeycomb of tunnels and a burial area for the royal family. At 203 feet (62 m) tall, it was the world's first skyscraper.

The transition from step pyramids to the first true, smooth-sided pyramids came under the reign of King Snefru, founder of the Fourth

As archaeologists explore the interiors of the pyramids, they can learn much about the lives and customs of the pharaohs who ordered their construction. While most of the items buried with the pharaohs have long since been stolen, the design and structure of the tombs themselves can unlock some mysteries.

The early Egyptian system of writing was called hieroglyphics and was a combination of word pictures and sound signs. Fewer than 1 in 100 Egyptians could read or write, so ancient scholars called scribes did most of the writing.

While a sarcophagus *(below and opposite) protected the body of the pharaoh, hieroglyphics (right) were intended to protect his spirit.*

Dynasty. Most historians view this time as the peak of Egyptian civilization. At a time when China had barely emerged from the Stone Age, Egyptians had invented writing and **papyrus**, developed new methods of **irrigation**, recorded the history of eight dynasties of pharaohs, and entered into the great age of pyramid building.

The Egyptians built most of the pyramids for their kings from 2630 to 1530 B.C. It is believed that the labor for building the pyramids came mostly from peasant farmers who were available during the yearly season when their farmland was under

water from the Nile floods. These workers were likely willing helpers, not slaves as some historians report. They may have been simply a labor force working for food and the hope that their king would continue to reward them even after his death.

The mummified body of a pharaoh was placed in a *sarcophagus*, or coffin, which was then placed inside a chamber decorated with **hieroglyphics** deep inside the pyramid. Buried with him were gold jewelry and treasures from his royal life, along with food, clothing, and even wooden boats to aid him in the afterlife.

STONE UPON STONE

No one knows for certain why a pyramid shape was chosen for the pharaohs' tombs. It is possible that Egyptians thought the structures to be holy since they pointed toward the heavens. Or perhaps they were meant to look like mountains, where the ancient gods were said to live.

Most pyramids rose from the desert **plateaus** on the west bank of the Nile River, where the sun would set. Egyptians believed that the setting sun signified death, and the rising sun in the east represented life. According to their religious beliefs, a dead king's spirit left his body and traveled each day across the sky with his ancestors.

When the sun went down on the horizon, the pharaoh's spirit settled into his pyramid to renew himself for another day.

The geography of ancient Egypt was perfect for the building of pyramids. The country was a long, narrow, fertile strip of land in northern Africa. There were harsh deserts to the east and west, dangerous rapids on the Nile to the south, and **delta marshes** to the north. These natural barriers allowed Egyptians to work in relative peace without fear of invasion or attack.

How the Egyptians managed the complex organization of labor and the physical movement of the huge stone blocks for the pyramids,

12

Like cattails rising from the banks of the Nile, the pyramids rise from the sands of the nearby desert. Whether viewed under a brilliant blue daytime sky or beneath the haunting moonlight, the pyramids dominate the landscape.

The most famous Egyptian tomb is that of King Tutankhamun (c. 1341–1323 B.C.), who took the throne at age 9 and died at 18. "King Tut" is the only king still buried in the Valley of the Kings. His burial mask is made of 22 pounds (10 kg) of solid gold.

Although King Tut's tomb was not as grand as the Giza Pyramids (opposite), the 1922 discovery of his funeral mask (right) sparked worldwide interest.

without the benefit of wheels or draft animals, is still a matter of debate. Egyptians may have used copper tools such as chisels, drills, and saws to cut the relatively soft **limestone** used for the outer walls. To cut the hard **granite** used for burial chamber walls, workers probably added an abrasive powder, such as sand, to the tools to make the carving easier.

The most famous pyramids were built on the Giza plateau, just above the Nile delta, from 2589 to 2504 B.C. They were constructed for three pharaohs: King Khufu, King Khafre, and King Menkaure, a father, son, and grandson trio who reigned during the 26th century B.C.

The largest pyramid, known as the Great Pyramid, was built for King Khufu, who reigned from 2589 to 2566 B.C. When completed, the pyramid rose 480 feet (146 m)—as high as a 50-story building. The Great Pyramid is thought to weigh about six million tons (5.4 million t) and contain two million blocks of limestone. The area the pyramid occupies could hold four of the largest churches of Europe, including the huge St. Peter's Basilica in Rome.

King Khafre's pyramid is next to the Great Pyramid. Although it is about nine feet (3 m) shorter than the Great Pyramid, it

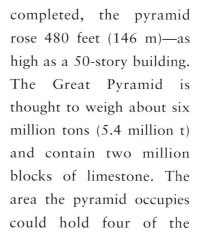

14

The average weight of just one of the stone blocks used to build the pyramids is about two and a half tons (2.3 t)—as much as two medium-sized cars. Some of the largest blocks weigh 15 tons (13.6 t), or about as much as five elephants!

Only the wind powered the feluccas *(opposite) that carried the pyramids' heavy building blocks up the Nile to their permanent location.*

appears taller since it is built on higher ground and has steeper sides. The pyramid of King Menkaure is the smallest of the group.

The Giza Pyramids were built on a flat area of **bedrock** that provided a stable foundation. Large rocks were cut from **quarries** nearby and to the south. They were floated up the Nile on sailboats called *feluccas* and then dragged to the site by teams of men using ropes and sheer human strength.

Workers trimmed the stones' surfaces carefully so that they would fit together tightly without mortar; workers wanted the fit so tight that not even a knife blade could be slid between them. As the pyramid rose, historians believe the workers built huge ramps that wrapped around the monument to help slide the building materials up the sides. Architects planned carefully to make sure the pyramids were strong and balanced. When almost finished, a special gold block called a "capstone" was placed on top. Finally, blocks of white limestone were added to the entire exterior for a luminous finish.

THE MYSTERY LIVES ON

The first known person to enter the pyramid of Khafre in modern times was Giovanni Battista Belzoni, in 1818. Belzoni was an Italian-born explorer, engineer, and circus strong-man. He managed to enter the pyramid and locate the pharaoh's coffin, but the mummy had already been taken by thieves.

During the rule of the New Kingdom (1570–1070 B.C.), pyramid building dwindled due to a big problem. Pyramids stood out across the desert like shining beacons advertising treasures to grave robbers. Goods were stolen from the tombs, and even some mummified remains were taken and never found. New pyramids were constructed with secret doors, but the break-ins continued. Pharaohs abandoned pyramids when they realized that these giant monuments of extravagant wealth could no longer protect their afterlives from plunder.

Instead, the kings commanded workers to carve tombs deep in the cliffs farther south on the west bank of the Nile—a burial area that became known as the Valley of the Kings. However, even this secure spot could not protect the tombs from grave robbers. The discovery of the nearly intact tomb of the boy king Tutankhamun (King Tut) in 1922 by British archaeologist Howard Carter hinted at the unimaginable treasures stolen from the valley and the pyramids.

Although stripped of their gleaming outer limestone by conquering Arabs back in the **Middle Ages,** the pyramids at Giza and other Egyptian sites continue to fascinate people. The pyramids are still among the largest stone buildings in the world. The Great

The tombs of the pharaohs have long attracted explorers and historians. Giovanni Battista Belzoni (opposite) discovered the upper entrance into the pyramid of Khafre. Howard Carter (center of top photo) discovered ornate treasures, including a throne inlaid with precious jewels and gold, in the tomb of King Tut (bottom).

Over the years, some people have suggested that the Great Pyramid and the Great Sphinx were built not by human labor, but by aliens. Another theory proposed in the 1800s suggested that the Great Pyramid was built by Noah, the figure in the Bible who built an ark filled with animals.

Near the pyramids, the Egyptians built statues of the pharaohs (right) and boats to carry them into the afterlife (opposite).

Pyramid covers an area larger than that of 10 football fields and was the tallest building in the world for more than 4,000 years.

It boggles the mind that men built these gigantic structures without the aid of cranes or bulldozers, and that up to 100,000 men worked 20 to 30 years to make just one pyramid. More than 100 Egyptian pyramids, many of them in such disrepair that they are almost unrecognizable, still stand today as the legacy of a resourceful and creative ancient civilization.

Scientists have been investigating the marvels of the pyramids for centuries, and

many new finds have been unearthed in recent decades. In 1954, a large cedar boat was found buried next to the Great Pyramid and is now displayed in the Solar Boat Museum on the south side of the pyramid. Five more large boat pits were discovered in the area in 1982. In 1995, in the Valley of the Kings, a huge underground complex of burial chambers built for the sons of the pharaoh Rameses II was discovered.

Today, Egypt's historic sites are among the greatest tourist attractions in the world. Many first-time visitors are surprised to find that the three most famous pyramids are not

22

Situated at the edge of the city of Cairo (opposite), the pyramids are surrounded by souvenir shops (below). While the influence of the modern world can be felt at the pyramids, the influence of the pyramids, in turn, can be seen in the modern world at places such as Paris's Louvre Museum (right).

alone in the middle of the desert, as it may appear in pictures. Rather, they rise up on the outskirts of the crowded city of Cairo like small mountains. Consequently, urban development reaches right up to the edge of the historic site. In the early 1990s, even a Pizza Hut restaurant opened near the pyramid square.

On the streets leading to the Giza pyramids, souvenir shops, **alabaster** factories, and papyrus museums compete to sell "ancient artifacts made while you wait." Each year, one of the three Giza pyramids is closed

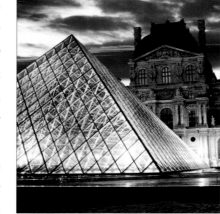

for a rest. Fortunately for curious visitors, there are always two others open to the public.

Over the years, the pyramid design has appeared in the architecture of other countries and can today be seen in such constructions as the El Castillo monument in Chichen Itza, Mexico, and the glass pyramid at the Louvre Museum in Paris, France. Although the Egyptian pyramids ultimately did not protect the bodies of the kings who built them, these magnificent monuments today serve the purpose of keeping alive the fascinating age of the pharaohs.

THIS IS STUART'S PLACE

KING HOREMHEP
ALABASTER FACTORY

SEEING THE WONDER

For the adventurous tourist, a ticket into the inner chambers of the pyramids—the only surviving monuments from the ancient Greek list of the seven wonders of the world—may prove rewarding, while others might prefer to contemplate them from a distance.

Few historic sites are as awesome to see firsthand as the Egyptian pyramids. To visit the pyramids, most visitors fly into Cairo, a bustling city of about 16 million people. They then take a taxi or bus to Giza Square, six miles (10 km) west of Cairo and home of the three most famous pyramids. Many people prefer to visit on Friday, when some of the souvenir sellers take a day off, making the environment a bit quieter. The best times of year to visit are the winter months (December to March), when the temperatures are milder. Tourist entry numbers at the two largest pyramids are set at 300 a day, so visitors are encouraged to buy tickets in advance.

It is illegal to climb on the pyramids, but an extra ticket fee allows tourists who aren't bothered by small spaces to go inside. Ramps into the pyramids are so confining that adults have to bend over. Once inside, visitors emerge into galleries and chambers with high ceilings. Almost without exception, tourists say the sensation of being inside these huge piles of stone is unforgettable.

The atmosphere at Giza Square can be something of a circus. Self-appointed tour

2 6

Although the Great Pyramids are the most famous attraction at Giza, they are not the only piece of history there. The site is surrounded by mastabas—which held the bodies of the kings' relatives and officials—arranged in a grid pattern.

Viewing the pyramids as they have been viewed for centuries—from the back of a camel—can lend a feeling authenticity to the experience.

guides approach at every turn, children peddle small statues, and stable owners ask passersby, "Want to ride a camel?" Visitors seeking a more serene experience can arrange overnight expeditions through the Sahara Desert dunes (sand hills) with a tour guide. Another attraction is the Cairo Museum, which is packed with amazing artifacts from the age of the pharaohs. Each night, tourists can be entertained as well by a sound and light show near Giza Square.

To travel to Egypt, foreign visitors need a passport and visa, documents that allow entrance into the country and specify the purpose and length of the stay. Sickness caused by certain foods is a concern in Egypt, and tourists are urged to avoid raw fruits and vegetables and to drink only bottled water. The number-one concern for travelers visiting Middle East nations such as Egypt, however, is physical safety. Visitors are encouraged to stay up-to-date on current events and to respect local **Muslim** customs.

QUICK FACTS

Location: Northern Egypt

Age: ~ 4,500 years

Composition: Polished limestone, granite, and basalt

Years to complete one pyramid: Usually 20 to 30

Builders: Probably peasant farmers

Number of builders required for construction: Up to 100,000 per pyramid

Dimensions of the Great Pyramid:

Area covered: 13 acres (5 ha)

Height: 480 feet (146 m)

Weight: About six million tons (5.4 million t)

Number of pyramids standing today: About 100

Visitors per year: ~ 2 million

Geographic setting: Desert

Native plant life: Includes date palms, sycamore
and cypress trees, roses, lilies, lotus, and papyrus

Native animal life: Includes camels, donkeys, buffaloes,
desert foxes, jackals, lizards, gazelles, and scorpions

GLOSSARY

afterlife—the time after a person's death; many cultures believe that people go on living in another form after their earthly death

alabaster—a type of shiny, white stone used to create ornamental objects

bedrock—the solid rock under surface materials such as soil or sand

delta marshes—flat plains between diverging river branches at the mouth of a river

dynasty—a succession of kings from the same family

granite—a very hard kind of rock produced by intense heat underground

hieroglyphics—an early writing system used by ancient Egyptians that combined word pictures and sound signs

irrigation—a system of supplying land with water (often through pipes or ditches) to help grow crops

limestone—a kind of rock made up partly of the hardened remains of dead organisms

Middle Ages—the period of history between about A.D. 450 and 1500

mummies—dead bodies that are dried and wrapped in linen bandages in an ancient preservation technique

Muslim—a person who follows Islam, the religion in which believers worship one God, Allah, whose prophet is Mohammed

papyrus—a form of paper made from the papyrus plant, a tall aquatic plant abundant in ancient Egypt

plateaus—large, flat areas of land at higher elevations than the land around them

quarries—pits from which stone used for building is obtained by cutting or blasting